A COLLECTION OF FRENCH-CANADIAN FOLKTALES

Old Grandmother's Tree

VOLUME 1

JOSEPH BOLTON

ILLUSTRATED BY NATASHA PELLEY-SMITH

Augustine's Alley

Cover and Interior design by Aaxel Author Group and Darlene Seong
Illustrations by Natasha Pelley-Smith

ISBN (Paperback): 979-8-9892325-0-5
ISBN (eBook): 979-8-9892325-1-2

This book refers to historical events and historical people in a fictitious setting within imaginative stories as referred to in the book's introduction. Other names, characters, places, and events are products of the author's imagination.

Publisher's Cataloging-in-Publication Data
provided by Five Rainbows Cataloging Services

Names: Bolton, Joseph, 1964- author. | Pelley-Smith, Natasha, illustrator.
Title: Old grandmother's tree : a collection of French-Canadian folktales / Joseph Bolton ; Natasha Pelley-Smith, illustrator.
Description: Leominster, MA : Augustine's Alley, 2024. | Series: Old grandmother's tree, vol. 1.
Identifiers: ISBN 979-8-9892325-0-5 (paperback) | ISBN 979-8-9892325-1-2 (ebook)
Subjects: LCSH: Folk tales. | Historical fiction. | Indigenous peoples—Canada—Folklore. | Indigenous peoples. | Farm life—Fiction. | BISAC: FICTION / Fairy Tales, Folk Tales, Legends & Mythology. | FICTION / Indigenous / General. | FICTION / Cultural Heritage. | FICTION / Historical / General. | GSAFD: Historical fiction. | Folklore.
Classification: LCC PS3602.O48 O43 2024 (print) | LCC PS3602.O48 (ebook) | DDC 813/.6—dc23.

This book is proudly sponsored by the Leominister Massachusetts Cultural Council in honor of New England's French-Canadian heritage.

This book is dedicated to my ninth-great grandparents, Miteouamigoukoue and Pierre Couc.

"Miteouamigoukoue lived a full life with dignity, respect, and love. A courageous and loving Algonquin [woman]."

— Father Elisée Crey, Récollet Priest, Pastor of Trois-Rivières, Québec, 1699

Table of Contents

Author's Note

I wrote these stories as a respectful and loving tribute to my ancestors and their traditions, both Québécois and First Nations. I do not claim to speak for any First Nations community, nor do I claim to be a member of any First Nations community. Furthermore, I fully support the rights of First Nations communities to decide for themselves who is, and who is not, a member of their communities according to any criteria that they should choose.

I am very proud to have both Québécois and First Nations ancestry, and it is my hope that Québécois and First Nations peoples will read these stories in the spirit of family, love and friendship.

Joseph Bolton

Editor's Note

When working with an author on polishing their manuscript, one of the most rewarding facets of that process is to see the manuscript grow and flourish. This facet was very prominent in my collaboration with Joseph Bolton for Old Grandmother's Tree.

To embark on an editor-author partnership requires trust on the author's part and a high level of dedication from the editor. In this case, Joseph was sharing with me and my team a very personal work, in that it was a tribute to his heritage, a heritage quite unique as an American connecting with his French-Canadian and Indigenous roots. At the same time, Joseph was striving to create folktales that were unique and fresh, while still respecting traditional parameters of such tales. The nature of this work was something I kept very much in mind as I revised and advised on elevating each story in the manuscript.

During this period, Old Grandmother's Tree expanded beyond the original group of stories, a testament to the scope of creativity that the book offered both author and editor.

There are so many elements in this book that the reader is sure to enjoy: A charming setting, characters to invest in, a celebration of family and connectedness, and, of course, important life lessons.

On behalf of me and the entire Aaxel Author Group team, it was a true privilege supporting Joseph through the manuscript development process as well as seeing this book come to life and delivered into the hands of readers like you.

Introduction

Folktales are ubiquitous in cultures all over the world. These deceptively simple stories that often feature fanciful creatures and trickster animals not only entertain but pass on deep moral lessons for living virtuous lives. Each culture's folktales have a certain flavor stemming from their origins. Yet at the same time, because they speak to universal themes of human life, they are appreciated far beyond the land of their origin.

This set of original French-Canadian folktales that are written by me and beautifully illustrated by Natasha Pelly-Smith has three main sources. The first is that I immersed my actual French-Canadian and Native American ancestors into a folklore world of magic and trickster animals and creatures set in the Québec of the 17th and early 20th centuries. The second source is the inspiration of Algonquin, Abenaki, and Mi'kmaq mythology. The third source is my own experience as a child of the great Québécois diaspora in New England.

I was born in Pawtucket, Rhode Island in 1964 at the twilight of the golden age of French-Canadian culture in New England. My 21-year-old mother, Carol Bolton (née Savoie) was the oldest of eleven children of Roland and Claire Savoie (née St. Goddard). At that time, many older French Canadians in Rhode Island could and did speak French. We even had French churches and French Schools in Pawtucket.

I was the first grandchild and was loved and doted on by my aunts and uncles, most of whom were still children themselves. In some of my earliest memories with them, I recall going to midnight Mass at Pawtucket's French church, Saint Cecilia's, and then on to my great-aunt's apartment for a big family Christmas meal. To this day, I still associate the strangely spicy aroma of warm tourtière with my great-aunts and with Christmas, in particular.

The rooms in my grandparents' home were decorated with crucifixes, statues, and religious art. My grandmother Claire would gather everyone in for family Rosaries. On rare occasions, I would overhear the playful French banter between my grandfather Roland and his sisters: Jeannette, Rita, and Florence. In many ways, I suspect that, except for the primacy of the English language, my early upbringing was much like what other French-Canadian children experienced in Québec in the early to mid-1960s.

I knew as a small child that we came from Québec. However, as I got older, the way I saw Québec also changed and evolved. In the beginning, Québec was the place of family legends and tales. My great-aunts would talk about their brother Georges Savoie, who, as Brother Donald of the Sacred Heart, taught mathematics in Sherbrooke and Drummondville in Québec and in Central Falls in Rhode Island. My grandmother Claire would tell the story of how her then-childless parents, Adélard and Eva St. Goddard (née Marion) visited the Shrine of Sainte-Anne-de-Beaupré to pray for a child of their own. My grandfather Roland would talk of visiting his cousins at the old Meunier family farm in Québec. They would also talk about how my great-great-grandparents Elphage and Delia Meunier would host Brother (later Saint) André Bessette for dinner at their home.

A bit later, Québec became an adventurous place to visit. My first trip to Québec was a family camping trip in Gatineau, right across the river from Ottawa. We visited the Parliament House, and this is when I became aware that there were two Canadas: one English and one French. We also took family trips to Montréal; the best ones were attending Montréal Expos games.

When my siblings and I were in our early twenties, my brothers David, Peter, and Patrick, who were fluent in French, would go bar hopping in Montréal. Their French wasn't perfect, though. My brother Patrick still laughs when he remembers getting yelled at by a bartender for his improper conjugation of the verb *boire*. Suffice to say that, at this point in our lives, Québec was the place for rowdy adventures.

Poignantly, my last visit to Québec, until 2022, was with my grandfather Roland and my brother David back in 1987. We went to Notre-Dame and the Musée des beaux-arts, drove by the old Meunier farmhouse and then drove a long, dull drive along the flat shore of the Saint Lawrence River for a quick walk around the Plains of Abraham, then on to Sainte-Anne-de-Beaupré. The trip was exhausting, and while I was certainly interested, I felt like I was an over-scheduled tourist. I feel sad about that now, at least in part because I miss my grandfather.

Many years later, with the advent of DNA tests and enhanced genealogical tools, I researched our family's history in Québec. The first big surprise came when I gave my mother and five of her siblings a DNA test.

Growing up, we were told that my mother's family was "100%" French. Well, it turns out we are mostly French, but the DNA tests showed that we were spiced with other nationalities, including Spanish, English, and Native American. Among those Native American gateway ancestors, I have found three so far. One was the Penobscot warrior named Madockawando, whose daughter married the irascible Baron Jean-Vincent d'Abbadie de Saint-Castin. Another was a Mi'kmaq woman of whom, sadly, not much is known.

But it was a third ancestor, my ninth-great-grandmother, an Algonquin woman baptized as Marie Madeleine but born as Miteouamigoukoue, who touched my heart. We know a lot about her thanks to the good record-keeping of the Jesuits and the research of the late French-Canadian genealogist and educator Normand Léveillée, who was also a Miteouamigoukoue descendant.

In 1652, Miteouamigoukoue was a young woman of the Weskarini band living with her husband Assababich and two young children, known as Pierre and Catherine, near Trois-Rivières. Her life changed forever when Mohawk raiders from the south attacked the settlement, killing and capturing many Algonquin and French people. Her husband Assababich was killed in the raid and both of her young children, along with a young Algonquin woman named Kahenta, the mother of future Saint Kateri Tekakwitha, were taken away to the Mohawk village of Ossernenon. She never saw her children again. Five years later, she married French soldier and interpreter Pierre Couc and together they became my ninth-great-grandparents. I was deeply moved by her tragedy at such a young age, but more importantly, I admired her strength, perseverance, and courage to live and to love again.

It is with Miteouamigoukoue and her husband Pierre Couc that I begin this collection of folktales. A good folktale will have a mix of literal truth and what I call folklore truth. The literal truth in these stories is that all the Meuniers, Pierre Couc, Miteouamigoukoue, Assababich, and Grandfather Charles are real people and are my ancestors, and that their relationships to me, and to each other, are also true.

In August 2022, I was already well into writing these folktales when

I was inspired to return to Québec. Opening a map, I saw a village just over the Vermont border with the intriguing name of Magog. A short four-hour drive later, I found myself the guest of Nicole and Michel, my hosts at the charming bed-and-breakfast, Au Coeur de Magog.

Honestly, I didn't know what to expect, as it was my first visit back to Québec since I was with my grandfather in 1987. Would I be welcomed? Would people get mad at me for my imperfect French? Would anyone want to talk to me, a total stranger from south of the border? It turns out I had nothing to worry about. The people of Magog were friendly and warm, and they were interested in the story of a French-Canadian coming home from New England. Even my attempts at French were met with benign amusement and encouragement. Thank you, people of Magog, for helping me to discover that the village of Saint-Honoré in *Old Grandmother's Tree* is as close to Magog as possible without being the village of Magog.

On that trip, I remember one warm, early evening on the shore of Lake Memphremagog, watching the sunset over Mont-Orford, as if I was experiencing Québec for the first time. I didn't feel like a tourist, nor was I a stranger, and as I walked over the land touched by my ancestors, gazed at the mountains that they saw, and looked upon the people who were literally my cousins, I felt love for the land and people of Québec.

I hope that you enjoy these folktales. I hope that you find them poignant, funny, and thoughtful. But above all else, remember that these folktales are a love letter from me to you, the people of Québec and to French Canadians everywhere!

Merci!

WITH YOU,
THERE IS A LIGHT

CHAPTER 1

A Late Winter's Dawn

Dawn, March 5, 1657
Trois-Rivières, New France (Canada)

A restless Grandfather Charles of the Weskarini band of the Algonquin people quietly sat up in his bed inside his longhouse. Despite his best efforts not to disturb his wife, her hand reached up and touched his back. "Charles, it's cold this morning, stay here and keep me warm."

Charles turned towards his wife. "You are going to have to make do without your big bear of a man this morning, Sehamou. I need to go outside and breathe in the cold air and hear the crunch of the snow beneath my feet as I walk." He began to look around for his winter footwear. "I also need time to think."

Sehamou sat up. "It's Miteouamigoukoue, is it not? I know you, Charles." Sehamou kissed the back of Charles' shoulder. "Are thoughts of our granddaughter making you leave this nice warm bed next to me?"

"Yes, that is true." Charles bent down and strapped his feet in a warm pair of moccasins. "It cannot go on like this, wife." Charles wrapped himself in an overcoat as he stood up.

"No, it cannot go on, husband. Miteouamigoukoue has been widowed now for almost five summers. But she is still young, and there are men in the village who would marry her, but she will have nothing to do with them."

Wrapping herself in a blanket, Sehamou walked over to the long house door. "The women are starting to talk about Miteouamigoukoue, and why she refuses any talk of marrying again."

"Yes, I know." Charles sighed.

Outside the longhouse, the red sun on the horizon created long shadows that crisscrossed on the rose-colored snow while a raven's caw echoed through the trees. No one was moving in the village except for one woman outside her longhouse poking at a few smoldering logs in a fire pit.

Sehamou turned to see her fully dressed husband getting ready to walk outside. "The sunrise looks beautiful this morning, Charles, perhaps I will walk with you." Sehamou's smile showed a deep love for her husband.

Charles shook his head. "No, wife, I need to do this walk by myself."

Sehamou laughed playfully. "Oh, so the warrior Charles is off to plan a mighty battle and to do mighty deeds this morning!"

Charles quietly laughed along with his wife. "You are more right than you know, Sehamou." He paused for a moment and then continued: "I am off to see the French this morning. Meet me in the center of the village when the sun is highest in the sky."

"I understand, Charles." Sehamou looked at her husband skeptically. "Are you bringing something back for me from the French?"

"You will see, Sehamou, you will see." Charles leaned forward and kissed his wife's forehead. "When we meet again, Sehamou, I would like you to bring Miteouamigoukoue with you." Charles smiled. "And perhaps you and your friends would like to pack a nice picnic for two people and have that ready as well."

"Hmm." Sehamou arched her eye. "Something tells me this will not be a picnic for us."

"You are right, as always, Sehamou," said Charles, "but I promise, we will do that walk together soon. But Miteouamigoukoue needs our help first."

Satisfied that Sehamou understood her part of his plan, Charles walked out the door and across the snow towards the French side of the settlement.

CHAPTER 2

Breakfast with Father Ragueneau

By the time Charles stood in front of the small village on the French side of the settlement, the sun was no longer pink. Instead, its cold bright light pierced through holes in the clouds, and its rays illuminated small patches of snowy Earth below.

The doors of the church swung open, and out walked Algonquins Magouch and his wife Tchiouantoukoue, Oumach-tikoueou and her husband Ouechipapaiat as well as French settlers Antoine and Anne Desrosiers, Pierre Boucher and Sévérin Ameau. They reacted with a mix of surprise and happiness upon finding Charles, who rarely attended daily morning Mass. Finally, Father Paul Ragueneau stepped through the doors into the cold air, still dressed in his priestly vestments. He smiled at Charles and grasped his arm in greeting. "If you are coming for morning Mass, Charles, you are about an hour late. But I am always glad to see you, my friend."

"And I am glad to see you as well, Father," responded Charles. "But while I did not come here for Mass, I would like to speak with you."

"Very well, Charles, but first join me for some breakfast and then you can tell me what is on your mind this morning."

Charles followed Father Ragueneau back to his modest home where they had a simple breakfast of bread and smoked fish.

"So, Charles," began Father Ragueneau, "what concern has brought you here this morning?"

"It's Miteouamigoukoue, Father." Charles glanced at the small statue of Mary holding a baby Jesus on top of the fireplace mantel. "She does everything that is required of her as part of our family and our village..." Charles paused for a moment. "But there is a sadness, a loneliness about her."

"She has lost much, Charles." A hint of sadness flashed across Father Ragueneau's eyes. "And she is not the only one. Ever since the attack... well, it is like we are all living under a cold spring rain."

"Sehamou and I see that as well, Father," Charles said. "We have had a good life together, Sehamou and I, and we want that for Miteouamigoukoue as well."

"Surely, someone in your village has expressed an interest in Miteouamigoukoue?" asked Father Ragueneau.

"Yes, but Miteouamigoukoue only walks away when any discussion of marriage comes up."

"But there does seem to be one man that Miteouamigoukoue seems close to, Charles." Father Ragueneau laughed softly. "But he doesn't seem to be in a rush to get married either."

"But that is why I came to you, Father, for you to compel both of them to do this," Charles pleaded.

"Charles, you must realize that they are free to make their own choices." Father Ragueneau paused and thought for a moment, and then continued. "Charles, my friend, I want to help you and when the moment comes, God willing, I will play my part according to my office." He looked out the window at the small church next door.

Father Ragueneau stood up and moved to the window. "My friend, I think you need to plead your case to an authority that is above mine."

Charles shook his head. "I do not understand the French obsession with titles and authority. A man has authority among his people because he is brave and wise, and the people know that he will lead them with justice. A man doesn't acquire these qualities just because a king grants him a title."

"Charles, you misunderstand who I am referring to. Follow me." Father Ragueneau led Charles back out the door and, in a few moments, they stood together at the door of the church.

"You want me to talk to Jesus?" Charles's eyes were wide open as he looked at the church door.

"That is correct, just go in," responded Father Ragueneau.

"It's been years since I was baptized, and I still don't understand: How can the Creator of the entire world fit into a small box in this church?" Charles looked up at the sky and swept his arm pointing to the vast openness all around them.

"Our words fail us, Charles, and no one has all the words we need to describe the truth and beauty of our existence." Father Ragueneau placed a comforting hand on Charles's shoulder. "What I do believe, is that he is there, waiting for you to speak to him. He also understands our sadness and our loss, Charles, because he experienced them both. Remember what I told you about Lazarus and the story of the widow?"

"Yes, I remember, but what should I say to him?"

Father Ragueneau opened the door to the church. "You will know what to say once you are inside."

Charles stepped through the door and then Father Ragueneau closed it behind him.

CHAPTER 3

An Appeal to a Higher Authority

It took a few moments for Charles's eyes to adjust to the darkness. The wooden church was simply adorned with benches in rows in front of an altar. On top of the altar was a gold monstrance with a small glass container holding a wafer of bread. Golden metal rays surrounded the glass container. On top of the glass container was a small cross. Standing next to the monstrance was a single candle. The only other light came from a few windows along the side walls. One window was open, allowing a cool breeze to flow into the church. Charles sat himself down on a bench in front of the altar.

"Hello, Jesus," Charles said self-consciously. He sighed and waited—should he wait for a response? Charles wasn't sure, but he decided to continue speaking.

"Father Ragueneau told me that you wept for your friend Lazarus when he died. I would like to know, Jesus, did you also weep for Miteouamigoukoue's husband, Assababich, when he died in the attack?" Charles waited in silence.

"Father Ragueneau also told me that you felt pity for the widow who was mourning her only son. Do you feel pity for my widowed granddaughter Miteouamigoukoue, whose only two children were taken away from her by the Mohawk?"

Charles put his head down into his hands. "Or do you feel pity for me, whose granddaughter, Kahenta, was also taken away, and who now must watch another granddaughter, Miteouamigoukoue, grow old, alone, with a broken heart?"

A tear rolled down Charles's cheek. He felt embarrassed by his display of emotion. No man should ask for help from a powerful chief with tears in his eyes, and certainly not from the Creator himself.

Charles looked back up and contemplated the monstrance on top of the altar.

I am talking about my own feelings too much, thought Charles, *this isn't about me, this is about Miteouamigoukoue. I must clearly ask for what I want for her.*

Charles looked up with a renewed sense of purpose and spoke with clarity directly towards the monstrance. "Jesus, have compassion for my granddaughter Miteouamigoukoue. Open her heart to love again, bless her and her husband-to-be with happiness and bless them with many children."

Charles paused for a moment. *Why should Jesus listen to me? I must ask him not to hold my failings and weaknesses against Miteouamigoukoue.*

"I know, Jesus, that I am not worthy to ask you for anything. I don't always live up to your teachings. Worst of all, my faith is not as strong as it is for other people. But please, do not hold my foolishness against Miteouamigoukoue, but bless her and hold her close to your heart."

Charles sat back and waited. "Do you have anything to say to me, Jesus?" Silence. Charles looked out the window, the sun was not yet at its highest point in the sky. "Well, it looks like I have time to wait."

CHAPTER 4

The Spirit World and a Strange Vision

Charles crossed his arms and closed his eyes while he sat on the bench in the church. His restless night finally caught up with him and he drifted off to sleep. No sooner had he closed his eyes, than Charles found himself in a forest. The sun was setting, and a strong wind blew through the leafless trees. Off in the distance, Charles could see a lake that stretched far to the south at the foot of a nearby mountain with three peaks.

Overhead the clouds rapidly moved across the dark, indigo-colored sky. The few stars that did shine flickered with the colors of the northern lights. Disoriented, Charles looked around to see if he knew where he was. *I have overslept and have missed my meeting with Sehamou! But how did I get here? And where am I?*

Charles suddenly noticed three young women moving along a road, struggling against the wind. To Charles, they looked French, but their clothing looked strange.

"Hello, young women! What village did you come from?" Charles called out to them in French, but they did not seem to hear him.

"Hush!" said a voice, "We must not let them see us!"

Charles turned to see a bear talking to him as he tried to hide behind a tree. The bear was the first familiar thing that Charles recognized in this strange place. "I know you! You are that bear Muin that steals our canoes and food from our village. Where is your friend Azeban the Raccoon?" asked a puzzled Charles. "And who are the young women that you are hiding from?" Charles gestured to the three young women walking in the road. "Did you play a trick on them as well?"

Muin smiled apologetically and shrugged. "Azeban and I haven't stolen a canoe in years. Do you know where we can find some canoes? We do miss taking them over the waterfalls."

Deciding that Muin was not making any sense, Charles turned back to look at the three young French women on the road when one of them pointed a stick in his direction. One of her companions also looked at Charles and Muin. Charles saw that there was something familiar about this particular young woman who was now looking in his direction.

Miteouamigoukoue? This young woman reminds me of her, thought Charles. But if she is not Miteouamigoukoue, then who is she? And why does she look familiar to me? I feel like I should know her. But how? He was just about to call out to the girls again when he heard a female voice behind him.

"Wiskijan! He should not be here."

Charles turned towards this new voice and saw a fox pointing at him while calling up to someone in the sky. Charles looked up to see who the fox was talking to and saw a raven flapping his wings, creating the strong wind.

The raven suddenly noticed Charles and then addressed the fox. "Oh, my, Wowkwis! I remember this man, he is Miteouamigoukoue's grandfather. I watched him while he prayed for her in a church, but that was many years ago."

"It's Grandfather Charles! But that was a long time ago! How did he get here?" Wowkwis turned to Charles with surprise and concern.

Wiskijan the Raven's eyes lit up with a realization. "His prayer must have gotten caught in the wind from my wings and blown him here from that time and place."

"Well, if you would just stop your incessant flapping, he should then fall back to the past where he belongs," said Wowkwis the Fox.

"But this is so amazing, Wowkwis!" Wiskijan the Raven was momentarily pleased with himself. "I did not know that I could do this, sister!"

Hmm, thought Charles, *so this is more mischief from those trickster animals.*

"Wiskijan! Wowkwis!" Charles shouted through the wind to the raven and the fox. "Why have you brought me to the spirit world? I have no time for your talking or for your tricks! Send me back so I can save Miteouamigoukoue!"

"Do what he says, brother!" said Wowkwis the Fox. "Send him home!"

Wiskijan looked down at Charles, slowed his flapping and let out a series of *caws* directed at him. Every *caw* though, became more human-like and sounded more like "Charles!" until finally leading to one loud and clear:

"CHARLES!"

CHAPTER 5

Charles Seeks Out Pierre Couc

Charles awoke with a start and found himself back in the church. "What just happened? Was I in the spirit world?" Charles caught sight of something black moving off to his left. He turned to look and was surprised to see Wiskijan sitting in the open window of the church, looking at him quizzically.

"Wiskijan!" said Charles as he studied the raven. "How long have you been here? Have you been listening to my prayer?"

The raven would only look at Charles silently.

"Why did you take me to the spirit world?" demanded Charles.

Wiskijan cocked his head to one side in confusion. "I have been listening to your prayers, but I did not take you to the spirit world. I have never seen you before today."

Charles was confused. "How can that be? I saw you there as well as your brother Muin the Bear and your sister Wowkwis the Fox."

Charles studied the raven. *Trickster animals are mischievous, but they never lie,* thought Charles.

"Wiskijan, can you at least tell me if you saw the three young French women?" asked Charles. "One of them looked like my granddaughter Miteouamigoukou, you must have seen them?"

"No, I did not," responded Wiskijan. "You and I were the only ones here in the church, and you..." Wiskijan pointed a wing at Charles. "You fell asleep."

"Wiskijan," responded Charles, "then at least take my prayers up high into the sky, far into the spirit world. Tell the Creator what is in my heart and do not let him forget my prayer."

"And who shall I say sent me?" asked Wiskijan.

"Tell the Creator that I am Charles, a man who loves his granddaughter Miteouamigoukoue."

"Miteouamigoukoue? Well then, perhaps my brothers and sister and I will keep a close watch over her." And with that, Wiskijan flew out the window and continued to climb up higher in the sky.

Charles watched him go and then turned back towards the monstrance. "I will be back, Jesus. Remember me, and if you do forget, Wiskijan will soon visit and remind you of my words. But now, I have to leave to do what I came here to do."

And with that, Charles walked out of the church and soon stood out in the center of the French settlement.

"Pierre Couc!" Charles cusped his hands around his mouth to amplify his voice. "I need to see Pierre Couc, and I need to see him right now!"

Charles's voice and physical presence created an immediate stir within the settlement. Men, women, and children dropped what they were doing and came out to see Charles and wondered what he wanted with Pierre Couc. Some of them asked, "Is Charles challenging Pierre to a wrestling match? You know how Charles is always looking for a new challenge."

Some of the men, however, began to fear the worst and thought Charles was putting together a war party to defend the settlement from another raid by the Mohawk. Antoine Brassard and two other armed men ran up to Charles. "Are we about to be attacked?" Charles could see fear, not eagerness, in Antoine's eyes.

Upon hearing the word "attack" some of the other villagers began to panic. Alarmed mothers began to gather their children. Twelve-year-old Marie Madeleine Hertel, whose father died in the last attack, ran to stand next to Charles, seeking protection. Charles and Sehamou knew the girl from when they would occasionally bring food to Marie Madeleine's widowed mother.

Charles put his hand on the girl's shoulder. "Madeleine, there is nothing to fear, go home to your mother."

The girl looked up trustingly at Charles and gave him a hug. "I still think of my father, Charles, and I don't want to lose my mother as well," said the girl.

"You are both safe," said Charles reassuringly. "Go home, my child. Tell your mother that Sehamou and I will visit soon."

As Madeleine walked away, Charles looked around at the French settlers. *Almost five summers after the attack, and they are still afraid. They need hope, and so do the Weskarini.*

"Everyone, please listen to me!" Charles held up his hands to get everyone's attention. "We are not facing an attack. This is simply a personal matter between Pierre Couc and me."

While Charles's words brought relief to the settlers, their curiosity remained, and they stayed in the village center to watch what would happen next.

"Now, who knows where Pierre Couc is?" Charles began to scan the gathered crowd for Pierre.

"I am right here, Charles." A handsome man of about thirty years came out to greet Charles.

"Good," responded Charles. "Walk with me."

"I don't understand, Charles what this is all about?" Pierre struggled to keep up with Charles's powerful stride as they headed towards the Algonquin part of the settlement.

"You will understand when you need to understand." Charles glanced at the young man with a half-smile. "But the first thing you need to understand, Pierre, is that you have called me Charles for the last time. From now on, I would like you to think of me as your grandfather, and I ask that you call me Grandfather, not Charles. Do you understand this, Grandson?"

"No, Char—" Pierre caught himself. "I mean, yes, Grandfather." Pierre was puzzled why Charles wanted him to use 'grandfather,' but he knew enough to not contradict him.

"Grandfather?"

"Yes, Grandson?"

"There are many people following us."

Charles looked back to the growing crowd of curious onlookers from the French settlement trailing behind them. "All the better, Grandson. In a way, this involves them as well, so it is right that they come with us."

"Where are we going, Grandfather?" Pierre had lived in Trois-Rivières long enough that he could see clearly where they were going but he hoped his question would prompt Grandfather Charles to explain himself.

"I am sure that you can see where we are going." Charles looked at Pierre. "Sometimes, there is value in silence, Grandson. This is one of those moments for quiet reflection and not useless blather and questions."

CHAPTER 6

Charles, the Wrestler of Hearts

For about twenty minutes, Charles and Pierre walked together in silence while followed by a curious crowd of French settlers who talked among themselves about what this could all mean. Finally, they arrived in the center of the Weskarini village to find Miteouamigoukoue and her grandmother Sehamou surrounded by many Weskarini people.

Charles smiled at Sehamou as he surveyed the crowd of Weskarini people gathered around them. "I see, wife, that you understood exactly what needed to be done, just as you always have."

Sehamou laughed and briefly held Charles hand. "You are a wise man, Charles, because you listen to your wiser wife."

Pierre lit up into a smile when he saw Miteouamigoukoue. "Miteouamigoukoue!"

"Pierre!" Miteouamigoukoue's and Pierre's reaction at seeing each other was noticed by Sehamou.

"I see where your heart lies, Miteouamigoukoue." Sehamou gave a knowing smile to her granddaughter.

"Do you mean Pierre, Grandmother?" Miteouamigoukoue blushed as she glanced at Pierre. "Of course, I like Pierre, Grandmother, doesn't everyone?"

As if in answer to Miteouamigoukoue's question, Pierre was surrounded by a group of young Weskarini boys and girls, who excitedly embraced Pierre like a beloved uncle coming to visit. This was not unnoticed by Grandfather Charles who, while not wanting to disappoint the children, needed them to stand quietly and watch.

"Children!" Grandfather Charles held up his hands to get their attention. "Today is an important day for Pierre, and I am glad that you are here to share it with him."

The children began to settle down and listen to Charles.

"Please stand over there, watch and listen."

The children moved off to one side but never let their eyes off Pierre.

"Grandfather, what is this about?" asked Miteouamigou-koue.

Charles smiled at his granddaughter but otherwise ignored her question. Instead, he turned to Sehamou. "So, wife, you have brought our granddaughter as I asked. Is the picnic ready as well?"

Sehamou nodded and pointed to a group of women who were busy tying up a large, full blanket. "Yes, the women are putting something together."

"Very well," said Grandfather Charles, "then I think that we can begin." Charles held up his hands and circled around trying to get everyone's attention. "Good people, both French and Weskarini!" People began to quiet down in response to Charles's booming voice. "I am glad that you are here today. I ask that you now watch carefully and listen closely."

Charles stretched his hands out to his sides. "Miteouami-goukoue, Pierre Couc, my children, stand here with me and take my hand."

Self-conscious of now being the center of everyone's attention, Pierre and Miteouamigoukoue shyly stepped up to Charles and each placed a hand within Charles's firm but loving grip.

"My children," Charles began, "your grandmother and I, and all the people here, have shared your grief these past five years."

Miteouamigoukoue let out a soft sigh, but Charles continued. "Grief has its place and its time, but now..." He looked around at the French and Weskarini people surrounding them, "we have all grown weary of living with fear, and living with sadness."

Seeing Miteouamigoukoue wiping a tear from her eye with her free hand, Charles turned towards her with a reassuring smile. "But today, that will now come to its end."

Miteouamigoukoue returned her grandfather's smile and subtly nodded her head. "All will be well, my granddaughter," Charles whispered so that only Miteouamigoukoue could hear.

"Pierre!" Charles now turned towards Pierre Couc. "Pierre, my grandson. I know what is in your heart. I see your kindness and tenderness towards Miteouamigoukoue. I know that you love her. It is true, yes?"

Pierre looked down at his feet for a moment before looking back up at Miteouamigoukoue. "Yes Grandfather, it is true, I do love Miteouamigoukoue!" Pierre, relieved at finally being free to say what was in his heart for a long time, spoke his words loud enough for all to hear.

"Well said, my grandson," Charles said quietly.

"And now, Miteouamigoukoue, my granddaughter." Charles turned toward Miteouamigoukoue. "Your grandmother and I know what is in your heart as well. We see how the fire of love is rekindled whenever Pierre is around, and we see how it is diminished in his absence. You do love Pierre, yes?"

Miteouamigoukoue gave a quick glance at her grandmother before turning to look directly at Pierre. "Yes, it is true. I do love Pierre, I love him very much."

Upon hearing this, all of the people cheered joyfully while Charles whispered to Miteouamigoukoue, "You have spoken well, granddaughter."

Charles raised his hands to quiet the crowd, "But this is not all, my children. There is more than love here, and your grandmother and I can see the deep attraction between you both." Charles looked from Pierre back to Miteouamigoukoue. "Yes, the attraction that is natural and good between a man and a woman."

"My dear Pierre and Miteouamigoukoue, this love that you share with each other and the natural attraction between you, this is a gift from the Creator." Charles looked at his wife and smiled.

He then returned his attention to Pierre and Miteouami-goukoue and continued: "Now, my children, I am calling on you to be generous with this gift, not only with each other but to allow this gift of love and attraction to lead naturally to children. Yes, children, who will bring joy and happiness not only to both of you, but for everyone else—for both the French and the Weskarini peoples."

Pierre suddenly blurted out, "But I don't know if I am ready to provide for a family."

Miteouamigoukoue looked at her grandfather with uncertainty. "Grandfather, I have already lost two children. I do not know if I can go through that again."

A murmur of concern and disappointment began to rise from the crowd. Charles, being a good wrestler, was well versed in anticipating his opponents' moves and was prepared for this.

"Pierre." Charles placed a hand on Pierre's shoulder and gestured towards the group of Weskarini children that mobbed him earlier. "We all saw how the children eagerly welcomed you when you arrived in the village. I have seen it with the French children as well." Charles looked deep into Pierre's eyes and smiled. "And why is that? It is because you listen to the children, you play games with them, you accept them, you teach them, and you love them."

Charles turned towards the crowd and continued: "Pierre, everyone here knows that you are ready to be a father, and that you will be a good one."

"I know that you are right, Grandfather." Pierre glanced over at the children as he spoke.

Charles saw this and gestured at the Weskarini children. A small boy broke from the other children and ran over and wrapped himself around Pierre's leg. Pierre gently roughed up the boy's hair and smiled at him.

Satisfied that he closed this objection from Pierre, Charles next turned to Miteouamigoukoue. "My granddaughter, all the young mothers here in the village rely on you to help them with their children. And why do they feel comfortable doing that?" Charles could see some of the young mothers in the crowd nodding in agreement. "It is because they trust you, and they know that you will not only take good care of their children, but that, above all else, you would protect them with your life."

Charles took both his granddaughter's hands into his own but before Charles could say any more, Miteouamigoukoue jumped into his arms and held him tight and quietly spoke to Charles. "I miss my children so much, Grandfather."

Charles returned her embrace and whispered back, "I know you do, my dear one. But you have so much love to give, Miteouamigoukoue, it will be the most magnificent sight for my old eyes to see you kiss the head of your child goodnight in your own home."

CHAPTER 7

A Walk to Uncle Mikcheech's Pond

Charles knew that there was one more important step that must be taken, and that it must be taken in front of everyone. "Pierre, Miteouamigoukoue, face each other and hold each other's hands." Charles stood before them and bowed his head and prayed quietly to himself:

Jesus, I know that my granddaughter will not consent to live with Pierre without a marriage in a church. I also know that Father Ragueneau will not marry them without Pierre and Miteouamigoukoue freely expressing to everyone that they wish to marry each other. I hope that you have heard my prayer, not for my sake, but for theirs. Open their hearts to saying yes.

Charles raised his head and spoke in a loud voice so that all of the people gathered, both French and Weskarini, would know what was agreed to:

"Pierre, Miteouamigoukoue, do you, in front of all the people gathered here, wish to declare your intentions to marry and to live honorably as husband and wife after your marriage? Do you both freely consent to this?"

Pierre and Miteouamigoukoue looked at each other for a moment before they both simultaneously shouted, "Yes!"

All the people immediately broke out into a cheer. Charles put his head down and quietly whispered, *Thank you, Jesus, and thank you, Wiskijan for carrying my prayer to him.*

Charles looked up, smiled and announced for everyone, "Pierre and Miteouamigoukoue are now betrothed to each other and next month, all of us, both French and Weskarini, will celebrate their marriage together."

Pierre took Miteouamigoukoue into his arms. "With you, Miteouamigoukoue, there is now a light in my life."

Miteouamigoukoue smiled at Pierre. "And Pierre, with you, there is now a fire that warms my heart."

Sehamou and two other women carrying bundles approached Charles, Pierre and Miteouamigoukoue. "Charles, I think these young people are ready now for some time on their own."

"Ah, Miteouamigoukoue, look what your grandmother and her friends have put together for you and Pierre to celebrate your betrothal."

"Yes!" said Sehamou. "In this bundle, we have put together a feast of good food for both of you today." She handed the bundle to Miteouamigoukoue. "And here are some warm blankets. We collected them from all around the village for you so you can sit on the ground and enjoy a quiet meal together." Sehamou handed the blankets to Pierre.

While the couple embraced and kissed, Sehamou hugged her exhausted but happy husband. "You did it, Charles!"

"No, wife, we did it together." Charles and Sehamou watched as Pierre and Miteouamigoukoue approached, carrying their bundles.

"Where should we go for our picnic, Grandfather?" asked Pierre.

Charles looked over to Miteouamigoukoue. "Granddaughter, why not head over to that pond that you like? You have loved that place since you were a child."

"Do you mean the one with the grumpy turtle, Grandfather?" asked Miteouamigoukoue.

"Yes, that would be Uncle Mikcheech the Turtle! I think he is quite fond of you, granddaughter, even though you always seem to make a mess of his pond."

"Who is Uncle Mikcheech?" Pierre asked.

"Perhaps I can tell you on the way," responded Miteouami-goukoue. The couple began to walk in the direction of the pond together, carrying their bundles of food and blankets.

Miteouamigoukoue began to tell the story. "When I was growing up, Pierre, I loved to visit this pond and throw rocks, poke things with a stick, look under logs and leave my footprints in the mud along the shore. It turns out that the pond belonged to an old grumpy turtle named Uncle Mikcheech." Miteouamigoukoue laughed at the memory.

"What happened next?" asked Pierre.

"Well, this turtle was so upset with my mess-making that he actually came to our village looking for Grandfather and wanted to challenge him to a wrestling match," continued Miteouamigoukoue.

"It must have been a short wrestling match, Miteouami-goukoue. Grandfather Charles is much larger than a little turtle," said Pierre.

"Well, you will be surprised, Pierre, by what happened next..."

Charles could see Miteouamigoukoue continue to gesture as she excitedly told the story of the great wrestling match between himself and old Uncle Mikcheech, but he could no longer hear what she was saying. *No matter*, thought Charles, *I know the story quite well.* Charles smiled at the memory, and then, clasping his wife's hand, Grandfather Charles turned to head home.

EPILOGUE

An Adventure for Charles and Sehamou

It was the next morning, and Charles was awakened by the early morning sunlight pouring through the door of his longhouse. As he lay in his bed, he reached off to his side and was surprised to find that his wife had already risen. Charles sat up just as Sehamou came back inside through the door.

"So, my big bear has finally awoken from his winter nap." Sehamou's eyes twinkled with joy and contentment. "Are you hungry? I have breakfast for you outside over the fire."

"You should not tease me so, wife, it was the best and deepest sleep I have had in a long time. Even better, my dreams did not include any strange journeys into the spirit world with mischief from trickster animals."

"You had a dream of the spirit world, Charles?" Sehamou became curious and concerned. "Tell me." She sat down on the bed.

"I will tell you later, but it happened yesterday while I took a nap in the church." Charles studied his wife for a moment and then smiled, remembering the events of yesterday. "But I would rather talk about our granddaughter!"

"Oh, yes," said Sehamou, remembering. "Miteouamigoukoue was so happy when she came home last night."

"Yes, she would not stop talking about Pierre. I think it was good that they spent the time together at Uncle Mikcheech's pond," said Charles. He had a faraway look for a few moments before he reached out and gently took hold of Sehamou's hand. "We should also spend time together, Sehamou. This morning, let's take that walk through the woods."

"Oh, we are going on a grand adventure?" asked Sehamou. "We could walk to the Great River or perhaps to that place where we can see the far away mountains."

Sehamou glanced around the longhouse. "I should pack a lunch for us too, a big lunch for a long walk with my big bear. What do you think about that, Charles?"

Charles inhaled her happiness like a fragrant spring breeze. *Even after all these years together, not a day goes by that I do not fall in love with this woman,* thought Charles as he daydreamed about his life with Sehamou.

"Charles? Are you lost in the spirit world again?"

Charles became aware of his wife looking at him expectedly.

"We can go wherever you like, wife, however, this walk must include another visit with the French."

"Back to the French?" Sehamou pretended to be indignant. "Are you looking to wrestle with the hearts of more young lovers among the French, Charles?"

"Oh, no! I would rather wrestle a whole village of Ice Giants, then put myself between two young people in love again." Charles laughed.

"Then why are we going to the French, husband?"

"Why? You should understand why, Sehamou. We must see Father Ragueneau." Charles' eyes twinkled with playful mirth and excitement. "We have a wedding to plan!"

OLD GRANDMOTHER'S TREE

April 16th, 1657
Trois-Rivières, New France (Canada)

And this is what they said...

It is a day of feasting and celebration. Today a young widow of the Weskarini band of the Algonquin people, born as Miteouamigoukoue but baptized as Marie Madleine, is marrying French soldier and interpreter Pierre Couc.

Pierre offers his new wife a gray shawl imported from France as a wedding gift while Marie Madeleine Miteouamigoukoue offers her new husband a wooden deer that she has carved in honor of their marriage.

Two families and two cultures celebrate together long into the night with feasting, storytelling, dancing, and athletic matches.

Miteouamigoukoue's grandfather Charles challenges his new grandson-in-law to a friendly wrestling match, to the delight of the wedding guests. Grandfather Charles quickly gets the better of Pierre in the match, despite his older age.

Someone in the crowd: I heard that Charles is the best wrestler in the village.

Another person: Pierre is in for a surprise; Charles is strong for a man his age.

Miteouamigoukoue: Be gentle, Grandfather, I may have need of my new husband later!

The crowd laughs.
    The wrestling match ends with Pierre's defeat and a warm embrace from Grandfather Charles.

Grandfather Charles: Welcome to our family, grandson!

Pierre: Thank you, Grandfather. Is Miteouamigoukoue as good of a wrestler as you? *(laughs)* I sure hope not!

The crowd laughs and cheers.

Grandfather Charles: *(whispering to Pierre)* I know that you will love my granddaughter with all your heart. Take good care of her and take good care of each other as husband and wife.

Pierre: *(whispering to Grandfather Charles)* I will love her always, Grandfather.

The wedding celebrations continue in the village long after Pierre and Miteouamigoukoue leave to spend their first night as husband and wife under the stars.

Pierre: Look at the stars, Miteouamigoukoue! There are so many on a clear night like this.

Miteouamigoukoue: As a child, I would often sneak out while my family was sleeping to look at the stars. I would try to count them, but I never could finish. Maybe they are too important for a mere human being to count.

Pierre: My grandmother said they are pinholes in the dome of the sky and that the Light of Heaven shines through them.

Miteouamigoukoue: That is what a wise grandmother would say!

Miteouamigoukoue: When I was a young girl, Grandfather Charles told me that the stars are the campfires of all The People who have died. They watch over their families on the Earth from the sky.

Pierre and Miteouamigoukoue look at the stars silently for a few moments.

Pierre: I wonder if Assababich is watching over us from one of those campfires. He was like a brother to me.

Miteouamigoukoue: My poor Assababich... he has been dead for five summers now.

Pierre: I often think about how he saved my life the night he died. Sometimes though, when I lay awake at night, I become afraid that I won't be able to live my life in a way that is worthy of his sacrifice... I miss him very much.

Miteouamigoukoue: Pierre, you are a good man, and you do honor Assababich's sacrifice by how you live your life.

Pierre and Miteouamigoukoue again look at the stars.

Do you really think that the stars are campfires, Pierre? And that our ancestors are watching over us from the campfires?

Pierre: I don't know, perhaps the stars are other suns, like the sun in the sky. There may even be other people on them, looking down at us.

Pierre turns towards Miteouamigoukoue.

But whether the stars are pinholes or campfires, I like them best when I see their light reflected in your eyes, my love.

A short distance away that same night, the ancient trickster animals of the forest gather to admire the stars above.

Muin the Bear: The campfires of the sky burn especially bright this night.

Mikcheech the Turtle: As the oldest of us gathered here, I have seen many nights and there is something different about this one, but familiar. Come to think of it, I have seen nights like this one before. The last time I remember a night like this one—

Azeban the Racoon: Look, everyone! I see a path coming down from one of the campfires in the night sky.

Puku'kowij the Moose: Does this mean that we are having a visitor? As the youngest one of us, I haven't seen as many nights as you have, Uncle Mikcheech.

Mikcheech the Turtle: Yes, that must be it! Now I remember! We are having a visitor from one of the campfires in the sky.

Wiskijan the Raven: Very few people from the sky return to visit the Earth. It takes many prayers to create such magic.

Wowkwis the Fox: Then we must make ready to welcome him!

Wiskijan the Raven: The father of us all would have wanted to be here to greet our visitor from the sky.

Wowkwis the Fox: Yes, Wiskijan. I also wish our father could be here to greet our visitor, but he is still in the north conferring with his brothers and sisters who live in the land of ice and snow.

Mikcheech the Turtle: True, Niece Wowkwis. It would have been good for my brother to be here, but he will return in a few moons.

83

Muin the Bear: But look, there is someone else coming here as well.

Azeban the Racoon: That beautiful girl? Who is she? I think that she must be from the village that we play tricks on, Muin.

Muin the Bear: Of course! She must be from there. We do have a lot of fun playing tricks on *The People* from that village, Azeban! Remember how we stole the canoe a few weeks ago? *The People* are still looking for us!

Puku'kowij the Moose: Whoever she is, I see a wounded heart that needs healing.

Mikcheech the Turtle: I recognize her, Nephew Puku'kowij! This girl sometimes visits my pond. Her name is Miteouamigoukoue.

Puku'kowij the Moose: Ah, thank you for letting us know, Uncle Mikcheech.

Muin the Bear: She is more than the girl who visits your pond, Uncle Mikcheech. I see her path now: she is the root of a tree that will reach the sky, and she will be the mother of many. For that reason, I think I will name her... "Old Grandmother."

Mikcheech the Turtle: *(laughing)* My eyes may be getting weak with age, Nephew Muin, but all I see is the young girl who leaves messy footprints all around the shore of my beautiful pond! She is a mischievous child, not an old grandmother!

Muin laughs as well.

Muin the Bear: My father gave me a special gift, a way of sometimes seeing paths that are hidden, Uncle Mikcheech.

Miteouamigoukoue wanders into the clearing where the ancient trickster animals have gathered.

Miteouamigoukoue: Look at all of you out here! Are you waiting for someone? Or do you like to sneak out at night and count the stars like I do?

Azeban the Racoon: Hello, Miteouamigoukoue! We have a visitor coming from the campfires of the night sky.

Miteouamigoukoue: I have watched the stars since I was a child and I have never seen the sky like this before. Are you saying that someone is coming down from the sky?

Wiskijan the Raven: You know him, Miteouamigoukoue. I have seen him watching over you with care and concern when I have flown up high among the stars.

Miteouamigoukoue: Do you mean to say someone is coming to see me and I know him?

Wowkwis the Fox: Have patience and stillness, and you will be able to listen to his words, Miteouamigoukoue.

Puku'kowij the Moose: Look, here he comes now!

Mikcheech the Turtle: Welcome to our home, honored guest who comes to us from the campfires in the night sky!

Miteouamigoukoue: Assababich! How are you here? I have missed you!

Assababich: Ah, dear one! How could I stay away from all the feasting, dancing, and storytelling from your wedding celebration? I wanted to share in your joy!

Miteouamigoukoue: It is true that I have married again, Assababich. My new husband is Pierre Couc.

Assababich: Yes! I am so happy to know that you will not be alone. He is a good man and he loves you very much. As your first husband, a life with Pierre is what I would hope for you with all my heart now that I am dead.

Miteouamigoukoue: He was always so kind and tender after you died. And I do love him very much.

Assababich: Yet, on what should be a day filled with joy, I see a little bit of sadness in your heart, like a pebble stuck in your moccasin while you walk.

Miteouamigoukoue: Sometimes, I still think of that terrible night when you died, and I wonder where our two children are. I still hear their cries as they were carried off.

Assababich: Oh no, dear one! A woman does not cry tears of sadness on her wedding night! We will have none of that.

Assababich: Miteouamigoukoue, a human being cannot have one foot on one path and one foot on another path. You will only fall on your face!

Assababich: A human being cannot walk down a path backwards... you will run into a tree! See, laughter is better than tears!

Mikcheech the Turtle: Assababich is wise. Listen to his words, my child.

Assababich: Now, grasp the hand of your husband Pierre and walk together with joy and happiness. Have beautiful and kind daughters, just like their mother! And strong and brave sons, who will make their father proud. You have a new path, Miteouamigoukoue. Embrace it.

Miteouamigoukoue: Will I ever see you again?

Assababich: Not in this life, as it should be. But I will leave you a wedding gift for you and Pierre before I go. Farewell, dear one!

Miteouamigoukoue: Thank you for your kindness, Assababich. I will try to follow your words.

Wiskijan the Raven: Fear not, Miteouamigoukoue, Assababich will still watch over you and Pierre from the campfires in the sky.

Azeban the Racoon: And we will see you again as well, Miteouamigoukoue.

Puku'kowij the Moose: Be at peace, young Miteouamigoukoue.

Wowkwis the Fox: Remember, a quiet and still heart can hold more love than a restless one, my daughter.

Muin the Bear: Go back to sleep now, revered and honored Old Grandmother.

Miteouamigoukoue wakes up just before sunrise. She does not remember how she returned to the campsite.

Miteouamigoukoue: Husband! Pierre! Wake up!

Pierre: What is it?

Miteouamigoukoue: I just had a dream of the spirit world.

Pierre: A dream? What kind of dream? Wait a moment, Miteouamigoukoue. Look at the shawl I gave you! It's no longer gray!

Miteouamigoukoue: You are right, Pierre! I can see the colors of the lights in the night sky! This must be Assababich's wedding gift for us!

Pierre: Assababich? How could he have given us a wedding gift?

Miteouamigoukoue: Yes, Pierre! I saw Assababich in my dream. He wants us not to dwell on the past, but to build something new and beautiful with our lives. He said that we will have strong and brave sons and kind and beautiful daughters. That is Assababich's wedding gift for us, and this shawl will always be a symbol of that gift for our family.

Pierre: You saw Assababich in your dream? But this shawl is no dream. It is real and it has changed color. How did Assababich give us this gift? Did anything else happen in your dream?

Miteouamigoukoue: Oh... and a strange spirit bear in the dream called me "Old Grandmother." *(laughs)*

Pierre: *(laughing)* "Old Grandmother"? I like that!

As the years went by, Pierre and Miteouamigoukoue honored the gift of Assababich by creating a new life for themselves and having children of their own. Today, Pierre and Miteouamigoukoue, along with their children, are celebrating their twenty years together with a family picnic.

Miteouamigoukoue: Remember the dream I had on our wedding night, Pierre?

Pierre: I remember how you woke me up from a sound sleep! *(laughs)* But I also remember that Assababich said we would have beautiful and kind daughters, and we have three, who are just like their mother!

Miteouamigoukoue: And two strong and brave sons that any father would be proud of!

Pierre: Our home, the children, our love—I hope that we have built the life that Assababich wanted for us.

Miteouamigoukoue: And the shawl. The colors remain bright, even after all these years.

Pierre: Perhaps you can pass it on to one of your daughters.

Miteouamigoukoue: *(laughing)* I am in no rush to give up this shawl yet, Pierre, but perhaps I can pass it on to a granddaughter.

Suddenly Muin and Azeban raid the Couc family picnic.

Miteouamigoukoue: Look, Pierre, it is that strange spirit bear Muin and his raccoon friend again! And they are stealing my pie!

Azeban the Racoon: We tricked *The People* again, Muin!

Muin the Bear: Old Grandmother's delicious pies make the mischief even more fun!

Azeban the Racoon: Tomorrow, let us go back to the village and steal a canoe for a ride down the river, or even over a waterfall!

Muin the Bear: More tricks means more fun for us!

Azeban the Racoon: The villagers will talk about us for many years to come because of our tricks!

It is the spring of 1902 and as Muin the Bear predicted, the tree of Old Grandmother had flourished and spread to the sky. A branch of that tree, Delia Meunier (née Gingras), lived on a farm in the Eastern Township village of Saint-Honoré, Québec with her husband, Elphage and their children Isala, Loyola, Adrien, Flora, and baby Arthur.

Loyola: *Maman*, Papa! Look at the Northern Lights! Aren't they beautiful?

Elphage: Yes, Loyola, we are fortunate to see them. It does not happen often living this far south.

Adrien: At school the teacher says they are caused by flares from the sun hitting the Earth's magnetic field.

Flora: I think they are angels painting in the sky with a big, *very big* paintbrush.

Loyola: What do you think, Papa?

Elphage: I think that Adrien and Flora are both right!

Isala: *Maman*, have you noticed that your shawl is the same color as the Northern Lights?

Madame Meunier: It is, isn't it? It is amazing how bright the color is even though it has been in my family a long time.

Flora: It's very beautiful, *Maman!*

Isala: Who gave it to you, *Maman*?

Madame Meunier: My mother gave me the shawl just like her mother gave it to her when she was married. I always admired it when I was a girl and so I was happy to have it as my own when I married your father.

Elphage: Delia, on our wedding day, your mother told me that the shawl has been a traditional wedding present in your family for generations.

Marie-Madeline Miteouamigoukoue

Marguerite Françoise Menard

Jean Baptiste Gaboureau

Marguerite Charron

Adelaide Charron

Delia Meunier

Isala Meunier

Madame Meunier: That's true, Elphage. My grandmother Marguerite told me that it was her grandfather, Jean-Baptiste Gaboureau, who gave the shawl to her as a wedding present.

Loyola: So, it wasn't only women who had the shawl. Perhaps I can have it when I get married.

Isala: Yes, when you marry one of the LaRue girls! (*laughs*)

Madame Meunier: I guess that is true, Loyola. But I haven't decided who will get the shawl. None of you children are even engaged! Besides, maybe I will skip a generation and give it to a granddaughter. (*laughs*)

Adrien: What I want to know is, where did it come from? Someone had to be the first in the family to have the shawl.

Isala: Yes, *Maman*. Where did the shawl come from?

Madame Meunier: Grandmother Marguerite told me that the shawl was originally her fourth great-grandmother's wedding present from her new husband on the day they were married.

Isala: The shawl was originally a wedding present? That's romantic! What were the names of the couple that had it first?

Madame Meunier: I don't know. What I have been told, though, is that the husband was a French soldier, and that the wife was an Algonquin woman from a tribe near Trois-Rivières. She was the first one in our family to have this shawl.

Madame Meunier: I wish I knew who they were. But even if we don't know their names, we know their hands held this very shawl and that part of them is interwoven into its fabric, just like part of them is in each of us.

Flora: Is it magical, *Maman?*

Madame Meunier: Of course, it is!

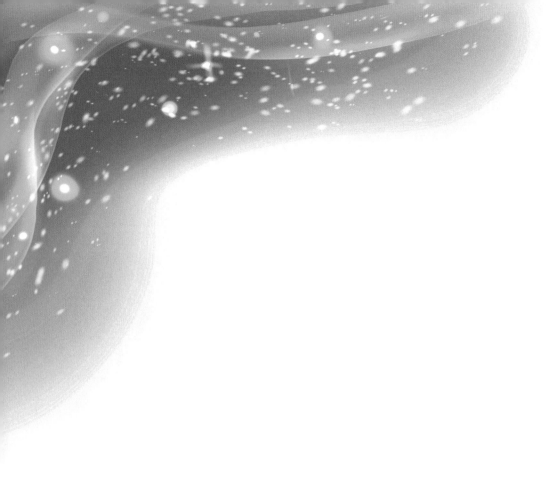

LA TROUPE DE
SABOTS

The Meunier Family Farm,
March 5, 1901

A blanket of newly fallen snow had covered the Eastern Township village of Saint-Honoré in Québec. While the family of Delia Meunier and her husband were asleep, their farm animals, who refer to themselves as "La Troupe de Sabots," were restless under the light of the full moon.

Claude the pig walked outside the barn and stood at the foot of Gingras Hill, looking at the untouched snow. The air was still and the full moon shining through the trees created dark shadows across the brilliant white snow. It was too much of a temptation for Claude, who felt the inevitable desire for mischief under the moonlight.

He walked over to Isabelle the goat, Henri the sheep, and the cows, Pauline and Hélène. "Hey, everyone, the moon is too bright, and I can't sleep. Let's go outside and romp around in the snow."

Isabelle was always receptive to Claude's mischief. "I love romping!"

"We cows are not going to be left out," said Pauline as she ran out the door with Hélène close behind. The rest of the animals ran out the barn door and jumped up and down in the snow. After a few jumps, Isabelle stopped next to Claude and looked up towards the top of Gingras Hill. "I bet the romping is even better up there," she said.

Claude thought for a moment, then said, "Hmm, I saw the Meunier children ride their new toboggan down the hill two weeks ago. It's here in the barn, perhaps we should take it up the hill and slide down just like the children did!"

"Toboggan?" asked a confused Isabelle. "What is that?"

"Let's go back inside and I can show you."

The animals followed Claude back into the barn and Claude pointed to a large wooden toboggan leaning up against a wall.

Isabelle walked over to the toboggan. "I know what this is. It is the floor that moves across the snow! I remember the Meunier children sitting on it and sliding down the hill." She tapped the toboggan. "They did look like they were having fun."

Henri tried to move it with his hoof. "How are we going to get it up the hill?"

"Maurice, of course!" Claude pointed to the sleeping horse with a red tuque. "We can put the toboggan in the back of the cart and Maurice can pull it and us up the hill. Monsieur Meunier put skis on the cart for the winter so we can glide right up to the top."

The animals walked to the back of the barn to wake Maurice. "He isn't going to be happy to be woken up," said Hélène. Claude stood on a box and lifted up Maurice's red tuque. "What do you want?" grumped a sleepy Maurice.

"We need you to pull us up the hill," said Claude.

"I need to go back to sleep." Maurice closed his eyes again.

"Please, Maurice!" Isabelle placed her front hoofs on Maurice's stall. "I promise to give you my apple the next time we get treats!"

Maurice opened his eyes and sighed. "Okay, we might as well go. I am not going to get any sleep with all of your nagging otherwise."

"Wonderful!" exclaimed Henri. "I will get my wine and cigars so we can celebrate at the top."

The animals hooked the cart up to Maurice, who then pulled it out of the barn onto the snow outside.

All of the animals stood next to the cart looking up at Gingras Hill.

"Is that where you want me to go?" asked Maurice.

"That's right, Maurice." Henri pointed to the top of the hill. "Up to the top."

Maurice turned and looked at the rest of the animals. "Get loaded up. The faster we do this, the faster I can go back to sleep."

"All right, everyone, let's load up the toboggan and get on the cart," instructed Claude.

The animals loaded the toboggan along with Henri's favorite red wine and cigars that Uncle Adélard Meunier gave to Henri last fall. Henri, Isabelle, and Claude then sat on top of the toboggan while Montcalm sat on Maurice's back.

Pauline struggled to get in.

"You cows are too fat to ride along with us," said Isabelle. "We will be squished!"

"What? At least let me on the cart!" exclaimed Hélène. "It's Pauline who's too fat, not me."

Maurice grew impatient with the realization of another possible obstacle between him and his sleep. "Cows, you will walk. If I can do it, so can you."

"You can use the exercise anyway, sister," said Hélène as the cows moved to stand along the cart.

"Is everyone ready?" Claude asked.

"I don't need any fanfare, Claude," interjected Maurice. "Point the way and let's go."

And with that, Maurice began to pull the cart up the hill with the cows walking alongside.

Arriving at the top, the animals got out of the cart and looked down Gingras Hill. "It's very steep!" exclaimed Hélène the cow.

La Troupe de Sabots took the toboggan out of the cart and placed it on the snow. No one seemed to be in a hurry to get on the toboggan.

Henri was also intimidated by the hill. "It does look steep." He then turned to Claude. "Are you sure it's safe, Claude? It was your idea to come up here."

"I did not pull this thing up here for nothing," interjected Maurice. "Somebody had better go down this hill!"

Henri's question gave Claude an idea. "Pauline, Hélène," said Claude, "please stand here on the toboggan while I inspect the hill to make sure it is safe."

"Why?" asked Pauline the cow.

Isabelle suspected Claude was planning some kind of trick on the cows, so she chimed in. "We need you to stand on the toboggan so it will not escape and slide down the hill before we can all get on, silly cow."

"I wouldn't stand there, cows," warned Maurice. "Claude's suggestions usually mean that someone takes a tumble."

Claude feigned innocence. "Maurice, you know I am always about safety first."

The cows, who were always trying to impress their fellow animals, never listened to Maurice's prudent warnings. So, the cows dutifully stood on the toboggan.

"Are we standing on the toboggan correctly?" asked an eager Pauline.

"I think that you are in the perfect spot, Pauline," reassured Henri. "But before we can inspect the hill, I have to get something important from the cart."

Henri took out the bottle of dark red wine and some cigars because he knew that laughing at the cows was always better with red wine and a cigar. Henri poured a glass of wine for himself and one for his frequent drinking companion, Claude.

While Henri was pouring the wine, Claude leaned over to Isabelle and whispered in her ear while pointing to the cows on the toboggan. Isabelle giggled and nodded her head.

"Claude," said Henri, "I have what I need. You can inspect the hill now." Henri made himself comfortable and lit up his first cigar of the evening.

"Thank you, Henri," said Claude. "I will now inspect the hill to make sure it is safe before we slide down."

While Claude was speaking, Henri winked at Isabelle. "Now, Isabelle," he said quietly.

"Have fun, girls!" Isabelle shouted, giving a firm kick to the toboggan. Maurice the horse closed his eyes, and the cows howled in surprise as they started sliding down the hill. La Troupe de Sabots laughed and toasted the brave cows on their adventure.

"Onward, my courageous girls!" cheered Henri.

"Pauline, why are we moving?" asked a panicked Hélène. "Claude has not finished inspecting the hill!"

Pauline tried to turn her head around to see where they were going. "It was Isabelle! She pushed us!" she shouted.

"Don't worry, Pauline!" Hélène shouted back. "Maybe we can inspect the hill for Claude!" Just then, she saw a bump at the bottom of the hill. "I think you should hang on, sister!"

"Hang on to what? Your tail?"

As Pauline finished speaking, the toboggan crashed into the bump, and hooves, horns, and udders flew everywhere.

The cows sat in the snow at the bottom of the hill while Henri, Isabelle, and Claude, still on top of the hill, laughed.

Pauline and Hélène, seeing that they were unharmed, were ready for another adventure.

"We want to go again, Claude!" shouted Pauline.

"Yes! We have finished your inspection for you!" added Hélène proudly.

Claude turned to Isabelle and Henri, who were still laughing. "Thanks to our courageous cows, the inspection is now complete. I declare that the hill is safe for tobogganing!"

Maurice opened his eyes and relaxed once he saw that the cows were fine. "But what about that bump at the bottom?" he asked. "I warned you all that someone always tumbles when Claude gets an idea."

"The bump?" asked Hélène. "But that's the best part, Maurice!"

"I want to go next!" said Isabelle eagerly.

"This was my idea, Isabelle," said Claude. "It's my turn now!"

While La Troupe de Sabots was busy arguing about who would ride the toboggan next, they failed to notice Madame Delia Meunier standing among them. "What nonsense is this?" Madame Meunier asked. "What are you all doing up here on the hill?"

"It's Madame Meunier!" said a relieved Maurice. "Now you are all in trouble, and I can go back to bed once she puts a stop to all of your foolishness."

Henri dropped the cigar from his mouth while Claude tried to hide his wine glass. "How did you know where to find us, Madame Meunier?" asked Claude.

"Claude, you are not the only one awakened by moonlight streaming through a window," responded Madame Meunier.

She then turned towards Maurice. "Maurice, take the cart down the hill and bring back the cows and the toboggan."

"*Oui*, Madame Meunier!" Maurice turned and began to pull the cart back down the hill to get the toboggan and the cows.

"It was the cows, Madame Meunier, they made us sneak out." Isabelle the goat was always trying to shift the blame.

"Don't worry, Isabelle." Madame Meunier smiled reassuringly. "You don't need to blame the cows for bright moonlight on the snow."

Madame Meunier then turned her gaze down the hill and watched Maurice as he pulled the cart back to the top. "I don't believe I have ever stood on top of this hill at night in the winter."

Once Maurice arrived back at the top, he noticed Madame Meunier's distant gaze over the fields below Gingras Hill. "What do you see, Madame?"

"Ah, my dear Maurice." Madame Meunier laughed softly. "I see leafless maple trees reaching for the full moon like dark hands, and white snow sparkling like diamonds in the moonlight." Madame Meunier then smiled at Maurice. "And I see a young girl playing in the snow."

"I don't see anyone, Madame," said a puzzled Maurice.

Madame Meunier said nothing but gently patted Maurice.

La Troupe de Sabots helped the cows from the cart and placed the toboggan on the snow while Madame Meunier continued to stare at the ground at the bottom of the hill.

A curious Isabelle pointed to the basket on Madame Meunier's arm. "Madame Meunier, what is in your basket? Did you bring some treats for us? I am getting hungry!"

Madame Meunier looked down at the basket. "Oh, I almost forgot!"

She clapped her hands. "Gather around, my dear ones! You must all be hungry after your mischief." She opened the picnic basket. "Here's warm bread and delicious cheese, a bottle of spiced caribou wine, and hot maple syrup to make *tire sur la neige.*"

The animals cheered and formed a circle around Madame Meunier. Everyone received a slice of warm bread with cheese on top. Maurice also had an apple because he worked harder than anyone else.

Hélène the cow spoke up while the animals were finishing their meals.

"Madame Meunier, you told Maurice that you saw a young girl playing in the snow. Where is she? Would she also like something to eat?"

In response, Madame Meunier turned and pointed towards the bottom of the hill.

"Did you know that my great-grandfather, Augustin Gingras, was the first farmer here, one hundred years ago? That's why it's called Gingras Hill," replied Madame Meunier. "My grandfather Antoine Charron made a small wagon on which my sister Victorine and I rode down this hill.

"In the spring and summer, the field would be filled with dandelions and blue irises. In winter, my friends and I would toboggan down the hill. We had a lot of fun back then."

Everyone was quiet, enraptured by Madame Meunier's story.

"As a teenager, my girlfriends and I would have picnics here with handsome boys on warm Sunday afternoons. I met Elphage here when I was fifteen. It was under that oak tree that he asked me to marry him. I was nineteen then, and of course I said yes."

At that moment, the bell of Our Lady of Perpetual Snows Church of Saint-Honoré rang out. It was 6 a.m. and the sun would be rising in twenty-one minutes. Madame Meunier turned back to face the animals. "All right, my dears, it's time for us to go home. I must prepare breakfast for Elphage and the children, and we all have a busy day ahead of us on the farm."

"But we didn't get to slide down the hill!" cried Henri, Isabelle, and Claude.

"We want to slide again!" exclaimed the cows. Maurice sighed. "I just want to go back to bed."

"But there isn't time, we all need to get back to..." Madame Meunier suddenly stopped mid-sentence and again turned back to look down the hill.

Hélène the cow noticed that Madame Meunier was again looking out over to the field under the hill.

"Do you see the young girl playing in the snow again, Madame Meunier? I wish I could see her!" said Hélène.

Madame Meunier didn't answer but instead turned back to everyone and smiled.

"Very good, dear ones. Elphage and the children can make their own breakfast this morning. Down the hill it is! Everyone on the toboggan for one more run," she ordered. "Maurice, bring the cart down the hill and meet us at the bottom after you give us a push."

All at once, the animals ran to the toboggan and began to tussle with each other for a seat.

Maurice's loud, grumpy snort froze everyone in place. "What are you all doing?" he asked. "Load the toboggan from the front to the back, one at a time, with Madame Meunier sitting up front."

Claude politely bowed towards Madame Meunier. "We are sorry, Madame Meunier! Please take the place of honor."

"Thank you, Claude," she responded as she seated herself in front of the toboggan. Montcalm the cat sat on her lap. The cows sat down behind Madame Meunier, Hélène first and then Pauline.

Maurice continued to guide everyone to their seat on the toboggan. "Let's not dawdle, La Troupe de Sabots, or we will be eating lunch on this hill."

"I am moving, Maurice!" said Claude as he sat next to Isabelle. Henri the sheep was the last to sit down.

"Why are you always the last one, Henri?" asked Maurice.

"Well, if something bad happens, I want to be the last one to find out."

Maurice sighed. "If you say so, Henri." He turned to look at everyone else. "Are we all *finally* ready?"

"Yes!" everyone said in unison, except for Isabelle who gave a loud "No!"

"What's wrong now, Isabelle?" asked Maurice impatiently. "Make it quick, you are interfering with my sleeping time."

"We can't go yet, Maurice, because Hélène is sitting on my hoof!"

"Don't worry, she won't be sitting on your hoof for too long, Isabelle," said Maurice as he gave a little push to the toboggan. "Off you go!"

"Maurice!" shouted Isabelle as the adventurers began to descend the hill, quickly picking up speed.

Seeing that they were finally on their way, Maurice laughed before dutifully trudging down the hill, pulling the cart and muttering to himself about how sleepy he was.

Moving faster on the toboggan, Henri momentarily lost his grip and almost tumbled off the back. "Isabelle! Help!" Isabelle grabbed Henri and steadied him.

"Hold on to the animal next to you!" she warned. "We almost lost Henri!"

LA TROUPE DE SABOTS

As they neared the bottom, Pauline noticed the rapidly approaching bump. "Don't worry, everyone, the bump is fun!"

"A bump? There is a bump?" asked an alarmed Madame Meunier just as the toboggan crashed, scattering her and La Troupe de Sabots everywhere.

"Claude, Maurice was right!" said Henri as he brushed the snow off his wool. "Someone always tumbles when you have an idea!"

"But you did have fun, Henri, admit it!" Claude's voice was muffled as he pulled himself out of a snowbank.

"Where is Madame Meunier?" asked Isabelle. "Is she all right?"

"Madame Meunier?" As Hélène looked around for Madame Meunier, she heard a young girl's laughter. Turning to look, Hélène saw a girl sitting in the snow. "Madame Meunier? Is that you?" Hélène blinked and now, in place of the girl, there sat Madame Meunier, still laughing.

Hélène moved over to Madame Meunier and lay down beside her. "It was you, Madame Meunier!" she said. "You are the little girl playing in the snow!"

Madame Meunier smiled and placed her hand affectionately on Hélène's neck. "You understand now, dear Hélène. I had almost forgotten the joy of a simple toboggan ride down this hill." She then turned to the rest of La Troupe de Sabots. "You are all such silly animals, but I love you all. Thank you for helping me to remember to have fun."

Hélène nuzzled her head on Madame Meunier's lap. "Tell us more stories of the olden days, Madame Meunier, when you were young."

Hélène closed her eyes and dreamed of warm summer days filled with yellow dandelions, blue irises, and little girls' laughter while Madame Meunier told stories of her childhood adventures on Gingras Hill.

MAURICE GETS
A MEDAL

CHAPTER 1

Spring 1902 in Quebec,
just north of Vermont

S pring had finally come to the village of Saint-Honoré in Québec. Blue irises and yellow dandelions covered green fields. Majestic maple trees, refreshed from their winter nap, stretched their limbs towards the warm sun, their branches bright green with new leaves. The hills cradled the little village like a caring mother and nurtured the new life within. All around Saint-Honoré, farmers were plowing their fields and planting the seeds of a bountiful autumn harvest for all.

On one of those farms lived Elphage Armand Gidéon Meunier, his wife Delia (née Gingras) and their children. That spring, the Meunier family welcomed a new member to their family, Arthur, who all four older Meunier children doted on.

Arthur was not the only new addition on the Meunier farm. In the red barn, Pauline the cow snuggled up with her new calf Mirabelle.

Pauline lived there with her sister cow Hélène, a strong horse named Maurice, a very dapper pig named Claude, a cigar-smoking sheep named Henri, and a mischievous goat named Isabelle. On guard over all of them was a one-eyed barn cat named the Marquis de Montcalm. The Meunier children called him "Monty" for short, much to the annoyance of the great Marquis de Montcalm.

As a group, the Meunier farm animals called themselves *La Troupe de Sabots.* Or in English, The Hoof Troop.

On a Sunday morning, the church bells of Our Lady of the Perpetual Snows rang out, inviting everyone for morning Mass. Elphage hitched Maurice to the wagon to carry the family to the village church while Madame Meunier gave the children a quick once-over.

"Adrien, button up your shirt. Flora, wipe some of the dust off your pretty shoes with this kerchief."

"*Maman*, may I please hold baby Arthur?" Isala, the oldest Meunier child, instinctively knew that her mother needed more help running the Meunier family home now that there was a new baby.

Madame Meunier handed Arthur to Isala. "Remember to keep him warm under the blanket."

Flora, at five years old, missed being the center of attention. "But I wanted to be the baby. Let's send Arthur back."

Madame Meunier turned back to Flora. "You are a big sister and *Maman*'s best helper now. That means you are getting to be a grown-up girl." Madame Meunier kissed her daughter and tucked her under a blanket next to her brother Adrien. Montcalm the cat sat on Madame Meunier's lap, as he always insisted on during family outings.

Loyola was the oldest Meunier boy and had hopes to have his own farm someday. "Papa, can I drive the wagon?"

Maurice the horse, however, who had led the family on this road a hundred times before, was not interested in ceding his important responsibilities to Loyola. "I know the way, and I don't need any help from anyone."

Elphage gave Maurice a reassuring tap and a smile. "Don't worry, my trusted old friend." Elphage then turned to Loyola. "You may drive, Loyola, just let Maurice do the work." Satisfied that his role as the real driver of the wagon was secured, Maurice turned back to the front.

Madame Meunier gave a nod to Elphage, who turned to his son. "We are ready to leave, Loyola. Tell Maurice to take us to the village."

"Yes, Papa. Come on, Maurice, time to go!" And with that, Maurice, with the wagon behind him, dutifully trudged on to Our Lady of Perpetual Snows of Saint-Honoré.

CHAPTER 2

A Stroll in Saint-Honoré

The Meunier family arrived only a minute before the start of Mass. Loyola helped his father unhitch Maurice from the wagon while everyone else headed into church, leaving Maurice and Montcalm alone in the village center.

Although closed on Sundays, Saint-Honoré's shop owners would leave treats for Maurice and Montcalm to enjoy while they waited for the Meunier family at church.

Jolly Émile from La Boulangerie d'Émile, with its heavenly aroma of fresh cakes, bread, and pies, would leave two Pets de soeurs (French-Canadian cinnamon pastries) for Maurice and Montcalm.

Kind widow Rosalie Fontaine of Fromagerie de Saint-André would never fail to have some slices of *Brise du Matin* cheese with two small cups of pale ale with which to wash them down.

Lastly, Maurice would always find an apple at Saint-Honoré's *épicerie* (grocery store) left by Monsieur Jean and Madame Patricia Bénéat.

Continuing down the street, Montcalm suddenly pointed to an open door to La chapellerie d'Éloïse.

"Hmm," said Maurice, "a hat shop, and the door is open. Maybe I do need a new hat, Montcalm."

With Montcalm on his back, a curious Maurice walked into the hat shop. The store was filled with hats of all shapes, sizes, and colors.

Maurice scanned the shop, noticing that nobody was there. "It looks like we must serve ourselves, Montcalm. Which hat should I try on?"

Montcalm pointed to a hat and then to a mirror on the wall. Maurice took off his red voyageur hat and replaced it with a woman's hat and then looked into the mirror.

Montcalm started to laugh and after a moment Maurice joined in the mirth. Maurice and Montcalm would put on hat after hat, look in the mirror, and laugh.

"Enough silliness, Montcalm. The Meunier family will be coming out of church soon." With that, Maurice and Montcalm headed back out into the street. Montcalm noticed that Maurice still had on a woman's hat from the shop as they headed out, but he thought it would be more fun to say nothing.

Suddenly, a voice said, "That's not a hat for a real horse! You want one like mine!"

Maurice turned to see a beautiful mare with a North-West Mounted Police campaign hat on her head.

"There's nothing wrong with my voyageur hat, thank you very much," responded Maurice.

"I've seen many strange things in my time as a police horse, and that," the mare pointed with her hoof to the woman's hat on Maurice's head, "is not a voyageur hat."

Montcalm laughed as he waved Maurice's red voyageur hat in front of him. Maurice pulled the woman's hat off his head and put the red voyageur hat back on. "Montcalm, what did you do?"

Montcalm was already too busy cleaning off some tasty bits of cinnamon pastry left over from La Boulangerie d'Émile to pay much attention to Maurice.

"Cammi is my name," the mare said, "and I am part of the North-West Mounted Police. We are forming a new unit to go way, way, *way* up north to deal with troublemakers, claim jumpers, and stagecoach robbers."

"Farther north than Trois-Rivières?" asked Maurice. It was the farthest place north he could think of.

"Oh, much farther than that," answered Cammi. "Why don't you come along? We are always looking for a few good horses."

Cammi took off her campaign hat and put it on top of Maurice's head. "Try it on and perhaps you will want to join us!"

Occasionally, Maurice would amuse himself watching the Meunier children reenact adventure stories from the Canadian frontier that their father Elphage would read to them. Wearing the hat transported Maurice to the Great North, the land of snow and unsavory troublemakers, and he imagined he too was part of these adventures and that he always emerged the hero.

"Maurice! Montcalm! There they are, Maman!" Adrien's voice brought Maurice back to Saint-Honoré. The three older Meunier children wrapped their arms around him while Montcalm crawled onto Madame Meunier's shoulder. Maurice looked down at the Meunier children hugging him. "I don't think I will be going anywhere, Cammi." And with that, he handed the campaign hat back to the police horse.

Cammi looked at the children and smiled. "Well, there, partner, it looks like you already are the hero of Saint-Honoré."

"We need you here, Maurice!" implored Isala.

"And since you are the hero of Saint-Honoré, you should take this." Cammi handed Maurice a wanted poster.

165

Cammi's rider, looking sharp in his red uniform, saddled up and said, "Farewell, Meunier family! We are off to catch the train to Winnipeg and then on to Whitehorse!"

"Have a safe journey to the north, Cammi," said Maurice. "I think my only adventures will be here in Saint-Honoré." He sighed.

As Cammi and her rider rode off to the train station, the Meunier family turned their attention to the wanted poster. "May I see that poster, Maurice?" asked Elphage. The Meunier family gathered around while Elphage unfolded it for all to see:

WANTED!
For Pie Thievery, Tool Snatching, and Overall Tomfoolery

The Pie Gang
Azeban the Racoon and Muin the Bear

REWARD!
$10.26!

"Ten dollars and twenty-six cents!" exclaimed Loyola. "With that reward, I could order that new bicycle from the Eaton mail-order catalog."

"The Pie Gang," Madame Meunier added. "The women of the church were talking about them. Everyone, it seems, has had a delicious *tarte au sucre* taken right off their windowsill."

"Some of the men have had tools come up missing in their barns as well," said Elphage. Then he turned to Maurice and Montcalm. "I expect you both to do your duty and be on the lookout for this raccoon and bear."

Maurice straightened up; he could be a hero after all, looking for this troublesome bear and racoon!

"Oui, Monsieur Meunier!"

THE DANCE OF CREATION

Dedicated to my younger brother Patrick Bolton, who
I used to carry in my arms when he was a baby

1970-2023

The Meunier family's adventures continue.

VOLUME 2

A heritage told through time.

A history of family connections, cunning trickster animals, and adventures untold; the second volume of *Old Grandmother's Tree: A Collection of French-Canadian Folktales* expands the beautiful compilation of folktales seen in volume one, set against the backdrop of early 20th century Québec.

On a frosty autumn morning in 1902, lumberjack Jacques LaRue enthralls the Meunier family with a strange tale of a mysterious forest giant inhabiting the slopes of Mont-Orford. So begins the next installment of the Meunier family's adventures as they navigate a world of ancient trickster animals and family connections.

Combining richly woven stories and stunning artwork, Joseph Bolton's and Natasha Pelley-Smith's *Old Grandmother's Tree* is a tribute to an untold history that will touch any reader.

Final Thoughts and Acknowledgements

I was very blessed to have great people helping me with the creation of *Old Grandmother's Tree*. Without them, this book would never have happened.

Unless you are an artist, you can't imagine the amount of hard work a large book project like *Old Grandmother's Tree* will take. **Natasha Pelley-Smith** lovingly brought forth over 400 full-color illustrations. At times, she was a marathon runner, working long hours. At other times, Natasha was a gardener cultivating illustrations like flowers in an exquisite garden. Her adventurous life experiences and personal journey of discovery of her family's roots have given her an empathetic understanding of not only my journey, but also of the characters in *Old Grandmother's Tree.*

Natasha's beautiful art, rich with dimensionality, color, and light, is brought forth from the depths of her wise soul. As someone with no artistic ability of his own, I felt privileged to watch her work and consider myself blessed to have such an amazing artist and person like Natasha as a co-creator of *Old Grandmother's Tree.*

Both Natasha and I are also very grateful for the work of storyboard artist **Masami Kiyono**. Masami and I have been working together on various projects and she has been a good friend and true believer in this book from the beginning. As the storyboard artist for *Old Grandmother's Tree*, Masami's uncanny and unmatched talent for visualizing the flow of story from written words on a page to a sequence of illustrations was a foundational work for *Old Grandmother's Tree*. Masami was the pioneer who cut the rough road through the wilderness for Natasha to follow and by doing so, saved years of work. Masami also created many of the initial character sketches for *Old Grandmother's Tree*, most notably the Meunier family and the Meunier farm animals. Her artistic DNA is sprinkled throughout *Old Grandmother's Tree.*

As a writer, it's easy to look at your own work and think, "This is great!" and "Everyone will understand this!" Good editors help us writers to see our first drafts as they are with all of their grammatical mistakes, plot holes and incomprehensive messiness. But **Alexa Nazzaro** also saw the potential of a great book when I brought to her my early draft of the first story that I wrote for *Old Grandmother's Tree: La Troupe de Sabots.*

I remember well our first Zoom call as I explained this strange idea I had for a collection of illustrated original French-Canadian folktales. Alexa's experience was critical to transforming what was an unwieldy collection of good ideas on to a solid foundation of a book that we are all proud of. Her coaching helped me to be a better writer and to bring these stories to their full potential. I am grateful for her patience and unwavering assistance without which this book would not have been possible.

An author's support from his family is important for his success. I would like to thank my wife, **Mary Bolton**, and my daughters **Rachel** and **Lydia Bolton** for their support for the many hours of work this book took and for being a willing audience for my early drafts.

I cannot emphasize enough how important my mother's siblings, **David Savoie** and **Ann-Marie Dau** (née Savoie) have been to me for their encouragement during those times when the scope of what I was trying to do seemed overwhelming. They both provided honest and helpful feedback for my ideas for the stories, and I am sure it was enjoyable for them to see the story of their grandparents, Phileas and Isala Savoie, come to life in beautiful illustrations and words.

This book was inspired by the late French-Canadian genealogist and educator **Normand Léveillée** (March 8, 1935- April 21, 2019), who was also a Miteouamigoukoue descendant and therefore my cousin. He did more than research the facts of the life of our ancestor Miteouamigoukoue—he brought forth a moving sketch of a real human being who overcame a tragic loss to rebuild her life. Sadly, for me, by the time I discovered Normand Léveillée and my own connections to Miteouamigoukoue, I learned that he had passed away just a few months earlier, having lived only about an hour's drive away from me.

Perhaps it was fitting that Normand Léveillée watched over the creation of this book from the Campfires in the Sky. I imagine that he stood there proudly, cheering me on while standing by the side of our ancestors **Miteouamigoukoue** and **Pierre Couc.**

I believe that there is universality in the language of our collective beliefs and mythologies. We all have different words that describe the same beautiful

226

truths of our lives as human beings. As someone from the Catholic tradition, the Campfires in the Sky is another way of expressing Heaven, where even now our deceased family members watch over and pray for us. It is both amazing and comforting to me that the belief that we are never truly separated from our ancestors is found all over the world. As Isala said in *Je me souviendrai toujours*:

> *"I think that all the stories are describing the same thing, something that is so wonderful that no one has all the words needed to describe all of it in just one story."*

In his research of Miteouamigoukoue and the Algonquin people, Normand Léveillée became acquainted with the story of **Saint Kateri Tekakwitha**. Kateri's mother, **Kahenta** was from the same Weskarini community as Miteouamigoukoue and was likely taken in the same raid as Miteouamigoukoue's children. Normand Léveillée had an intuitive sense that Kahenta and Miteouamigoukoue were possibly related. Although there is no record of a family connection, I personally felt that Saint Kateri was watching over this book as it was created. I certainly always had the resources that I needed for this book when I needed them as well as the support of the right people.

Additionally, at times it seemed that Miteouamigoukoue, Pierre Couc, and **Assababich** directly inspired how they were portrayed in these stories. I cannot explain or describe how that is true, but it felt that it was real. As I have pondered that, I realized that both Miteouamigoukoue and Saint Kateri experienced tragic losses of family members in their lives, and that it would make perfect sense for them to still be lovingly interested in and concerned for their family living today in the 21st century.

As I write these words, I realize that there are still other stories to tell from the world of Old Grandmother's Tree:

- Where did the ancient trickster animals come from and how did they first meet The People?
- What was the friendship between Miteouamigoukoue and Mikcheech?
- Who won the legendary wrestling match between Grandfather Charles and Mikcheech?
- What happened during the tug-of-war between the Meunier farm

animals and the LaRue farm animals?

- How did Gaëlle and Maëlle LaRue meet their husbands in Whitehorse? And why are they being chased by a flying canoe?
- Who are the other trickster animals?
- What did Aunt Victorine and Adrien find at the top of Mont-Orford?

A writer's work is never done. I am planning on working through these stories over the next couple of years and you will be able to find them on my website. I hope that you enjoyed these folktales and if you did, please consider giving or sharing a copy of this book to others who may enjoy them. More than ever, we need good stories to read to ourselves and to each other.

Merci!

Artist Statement
by Natasha Pelley-Smith

Being a part of this book has been a profound honor. Collaborating with Joseph, the author and co-creator, has been an enriching experience as we bring each illustration to life. Together, we've witnessed the emergence of a powerful collective of stories that form a cohesive whole—an anticipation that I am eager to share with others.

Throughout the creative process, I've utilized a graphic monitor tablet, allowing me to draw with the same authenticity as I would on paper. This method enhances the hand-drawn quality, and I hope readers will appreciate the tangible connection it brings to the artwork. Drawing inspiration from the talented storyboard artist Masami, I integrated Joe's vision and historical research into my work as well as my own ideas. Adapting from detailed notes, I crafted a vibrant and unique style that adds a captivating pop to the illustrations.

Lighting holds a special significance in my artistic process, serving as a crucial element to breathe life into the characters. It's also my favorite stage to refine, providing a finishing touch that enhances the overall visual experience.

Reflecting on the journey of illustrating this book, I never anticipated the long journey it would take. However, time seems to fly and I find myself captivated by the unfolding narrative every day I draw. I believe that future readers will share in this immersive experience, feeling time slip away as they delve into the captivating stories that transport them to another world.

About the Author

Joseph Bolton was born in Pawtucket, Rhode Island during the twilight of the golden age of French-Canadian culture in New England. Growing up emersed in his mother's French-Canadian family, Joseph enjoyed hearing the stories told by his grandparents and great aunts of a mysterious and magical place called Québec, otherwise known as "the place we came from."

After high school, Joseph's adventurous nature led him to enlist in the U.S. Army and he served in the Army's airborne forces as a paratrooper jumping out of perfectly good airplanes, much to the worry of his mother.

Although he originally intended to stay in the Army for two years, he was appointed to the United States Military Academy at West Point, and after graduating in 1989, he decided to make the Army a career. After West Point, Joseph graduated from the Army's Ranger Training School, a grueling and physically demanding combat leadership course. Over the next 18 years, Joseph served in the army in various positions of growing responsibilities culminating with a combat tour in Afghanistan as one of two Space Operations Officers with the US Army's 10th Mountain Division.

Since he retired from the Army, Joseph has worked in various project manager roles as a civilian contractor for the U.S. Air Force. While writing Old Grandmother's Tree, Joseph took a sabbatical from the U.S. Air Force and taught mathematics to young students for a semester at Holy Family Academy in Gardner Massachusetts. He considers it the most fulfilling job he has ever had and hopes to return to teaching full-time in the near future.

Bolton is of French-Canadian, Native American, Spanish, English, and Irish descent, and is profoundly inspired by the stories of his heritage. He lives with his wife in Massachusetts, and, in his free time, enjoys hiking and skiing through Québec and New England landscapes. His favorite places to go for outdoor adventure are the Berkshire Mountains of Massachusetts and Mont-Orford in Québec. When he is not writing, hiking, or skiing, Joseph enjoys reading about science, history, philosophy, mathematics, and worldwide mythologies. *Old Grandmother's Tree* is his first book.

About the Illustrator

Natasha Pelley-Smith, born in Toronto, is a seasoned professional artist who graduated from the prestigious Écohlcité fine arts academy in France, in 2017—now integrated into Émile Chol of Lyon. Equipped with a diverse skill set that spans from crafting murals of all sizes to illustrating books and creating canvas paintings in oils, acrylics and mixed media, Natasha's professional journey is a continual creative adventure.

Her artistic focal point revolves around expressive portraiture, wherein she delves into the realms of self-identity exploration and cultural influences. Natasha is known to embody her Native-American, Jamaican, and Newfoundland roots, as well as other cultural threads from her life. Her work serves as an invitation for others to embrace their multi-faceted layers, both culturally and emotionally, promoting messages of unity and self-love.

Having returned to her Canadian roots, Natasha continues to make significant contributions in mural painting, canvas art, and illustration. Throughout her career, she has collaborated artistically with renowned commercial companies such as CiteCreation in France and Canadian/US companies like Lycopodium Minerals Canada Ltd., Randstad Canada, the City of Pickering, Longslice Brewery, Black Calder Brewery Co., York Regional Bell Box, the City of Richmond Hill in Ontario, as well as the bubble tea restaurant, Nuttea Toronto. Many of these projects displayed ties with diversity, cultural and environmental aspects.

Natasha's private clientele is also noteworthy, where her artwork has garnered recognition, including four fully illustrated published books, leading to her collaboration with U.S. author Joseph Bolton on her most extensive project to date. This book intricately dives into French-Canadian folklore, character self-growth and prominently explores Joseph's heritage and Native American roots from the Algonquin tribes while also embracing the unified connection to Natasha's roots from the Ojibwe, Kootenay and Cree tribes, featured subtly throughout the book.

Natasha continues to immerse herself in illustrating *Old Grandmother's Tree*, a series that will continue to unfold as a symbol of Indigenous culture to cherish. For a glimpse into Natasha's individual artistry, her work can be explored at:
welcome.natashapsartwork.ca/

About the Storyboard Artist

Masami F. Kiyono is a biracial Japanese American illustrator and storyboard artist who has worked on projects ranging from children's storybooks to Superbowl commercials. One of her latest projects includes creating illustrations for a documentary titled Voices of Deoli (2024), which tells the story of how roughly 3,000 Chinese Indians were imprisoned in internment camps after the Sino-Indian War, and how the remaining survivors manage to thrive today.

In her free time, Masami enjoys watching cartoons and learning about folklore. These interests along with her cultural background influence her work, often containing dark whimsy and a bit of humor.

Masami has been working with Joseph Bolton since the beginning of this project and has seen it evolve significantly. What started as a sweet story about magical barnyard animals revealed itself to be a personal retelling of the writer's family history. It was at this point that the visual planning and storyboarding for the project began to focus on world-building. The characters and their environments had to reflect the underlying magic continuously present throughout the province; everything down to the color of Delia Meunier's shawl became connected to the celestial powers that influenced events throughout the story. It's this kind of planning that excites Masami the most when illustrating a story, which is why she eagerly took on the challenge.

To see more of her illustration work, you can visit her website at: **masamikiyono.com/illustrations.**

Made in the USA
Middletown, DE
23 August 2024

59569099R00139